For Karin

—M. G. L.

For my beloved Checo, with thanks for everything,
and for his granddaughter, my sweet and dear Miranda

—C. V.

flyaway
books

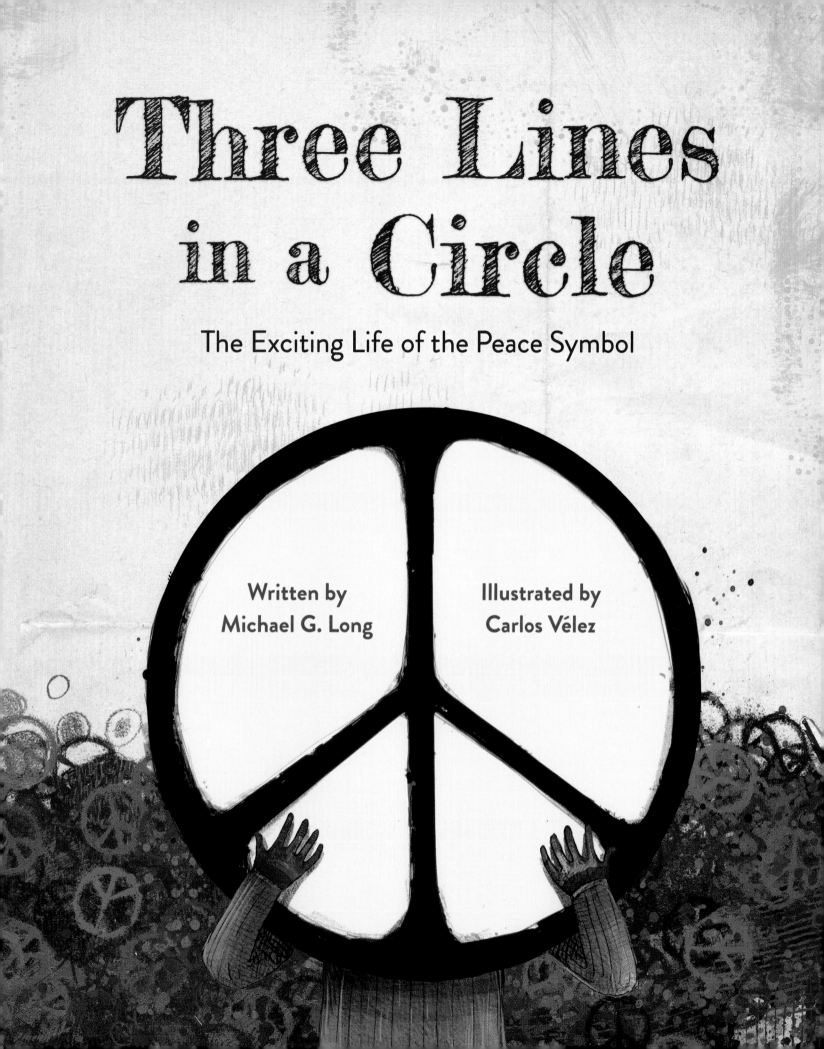

Three Lines in a Circle

The Exciting Life of the Peace Symbol

Written by
Michael G. Long

Illustrated by
Carlos Vélez

Gerry hovered over his drafting table
and began to draw his dream.

One line
straight down.

One line
to the right.

One line
to the left,
then a circle.
That was all—
just three lines
in a circle.

That's it! Gerry thought.
*A symbol of my dream—
a world without bombs.*

Energized and excited,
Gerry asked people
who shared his dream
to share his design
with others who
shared their dream.

But one man mocked it, saying,
"It doesn't mean a thing,
and it will *never* catch on."

Wow—

was he ever wrong!

It caught on
all over London
and all over England,
standing for

BAN THE BOMB!

CND

NO WAR

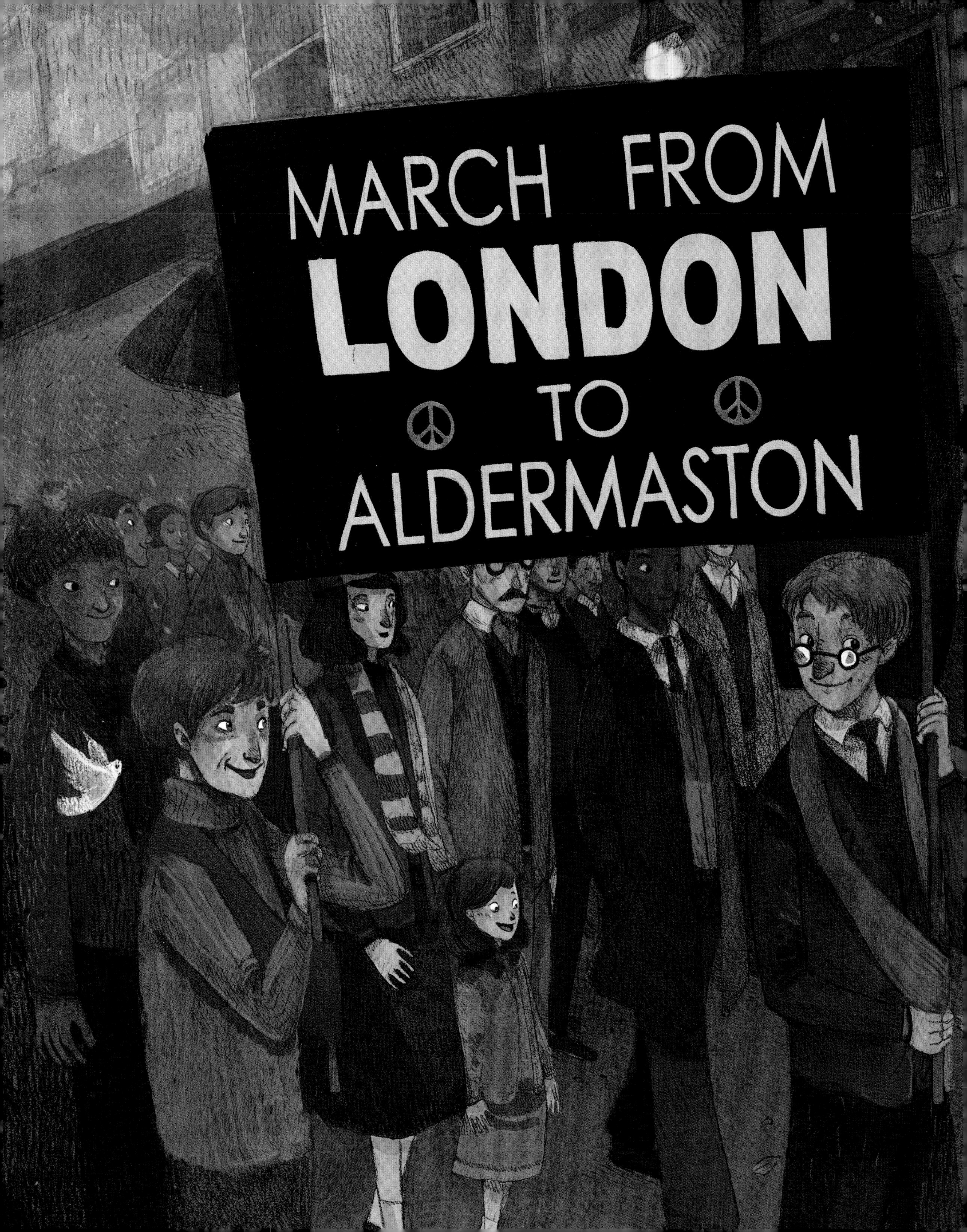
MARCH FROM
LONDON
TO
ALDERMASTON

It sailed on
to the United States of America,
where it also caught on,
standing for

MAKE PEACE
NOT WAR!

Yes, indeed—
it caught on
and on and on,
standing for

peace

for all
and especially for

Black people
and
Brown people,

women
and
poor people,

LGBTQ+ people
and
people with disabilities.

It sailed on
across the globe,
where it caught on,
standing for

PEACE

for all

and especially for . . .

Black people in South Africa,
unity in Germany,
Aboriginal people in Australia.

WE ARE
ALL
ONE

Oh, my—
how it caught on
and on and on,
standing for . . .

PEACE

for all
and especially for

Earth
and animals
and fish.

It caught on
and on,
until today,
when it stands for . . .

PRIDE

NO FUTURE WITHOUT NATURE

PEACE

and

END GUN VIOLENCE!

PEACE

and

BLACK LIVES MATTER!

SAVE THE WORLD

PEACE
and
BELIEVE
WOMEN!

PEACE
and
STOP CLIMATE
CHANGE!

THREE
LINES
IN A CIRCLE,

catching on,

fighting on,

moving on . . .

TO YOU.

A
SHORT HISTORY
of the
PEACE SYMBOL

Near the end of February in 1958, Gerald Holtom, a graphic design artist and a former conscientious objector, attended an early evening meeting of the Direct Action Committee against Nuclear War (DAC) in South London. The committee's three members—Hugh Brock, Pat Arrowsmith, and Michael Randle—were planning a protest march against nuclear weapons. The fifty-mile-long march was to start in London on Good Friday and end on Easter Sunday at a nuclear weapons factory in Aldermaston.

"So, Gerry, let's see what you have for us," said Brock.

Holtom opened his portfolio and pulled out his pictures. "I've tried a simple approach," he said, pointing to the three lines in a circle.

He explained that when drawing the symbol, he adopted letters from semaphore, the alphabet used by people sending messages by flags. The two lines pointing downward and to the sides came from the semaphore letter for *N*, and the center line represented the letter *D*. Placed on top of each other and enclosed in a circle, the three lines stood for "nuclear disarmament."

After the meeting, Randle showed the symbol to a colleague in the peace movement. "What on earth were you three thinking?" said the bewildered man. "It doesn't mean a thing, and it will never catch on."

Back in his West London studio, Holtom produced black and white banners displaying his symbol in gold leaf so that it would reflect car headlights during the evening hours of the march. He also enlisted his staff and children to help silk-screen five hundred picket signs—he called them "lollipops"—featuring the symbol in different colors. About half of the symbols were black and white; they were to be used on Good Friday and Saturday. The other half were green and white, for use on Easter Sunday. The change in colors would represent transformation—from winter to spring and from death to life.

The symbol debuted in public on April 4, 1958, at the kickoff for the march from London to Aldermaston. At the front of the protest was a banner that included two peace symbols. Lollipop peace signs, as well as other peace banners, were also raised high among the five hundred to six hundred marchers.

Ten days later, a photograph of the protest appeared in *Life*, a popular magazine based in the United States. Peace historian Ken Kolsbun believes that the publication of this photograph marked the first time that the symbol migrated from England to the United States.

Back in Europe, the symbol soon became widespread among the growing number of antinuclear activists, appearing on clothes, flags, banners, buttons—anywhere someone wanted to share its message about disarmament. Neither Holtom nor the disarmament committee sought to copyright the symbol; they put no legal restrictions on its use. They wanted everyone to have free and open access to it.

It took a few more years for the symbol to become prominent in the United States. In 1960, the Committee for Nonviolent Action (CNVA), a group opposed to nuclear weapons, used the symbol on flyers and on signs that activists carried on the San Francisco to Moscow Walk for Peace, which began in December 1960 and ended in October 1961.

But the symbol's popularity increased beyond measure when U.S.-based activists began to use it in their protests against the Vietnam War. Antiwar activists, especially students, sewed patches of the symbol onto their shirts, jackets, and jeans. It appeared everywhere someone wanted to declare opposition to the Vietnam War. In the United States, the nuclear disarmament symbol became the peace symbol, and it began to spread throughout the Black civil rights movement, especially when Martin Luther King Jr. and other leaders criticized President Johnson for using more money to fight the Vietnam War than to help poor people in the United States. Other social movements also began to adopt the symbol for their own campaigns: women's rights, the environment, LGBTQ+ rights, and more.

Gerald Holtom died in 1985, having lived to see his nuclear disarmament symbol—our peace symbol—take root across the globe, where it continues to inspire all of us involved in the fight for peace, justice, and equality.

A Partial Time Line of Peaceful Protests since 1958

1958   London to Aldermaston (England) march against nuclear weapons

1960   San Francisco to Moscow Walk for Peace

1961   Freedom Rides by activists opposed to segregation in interstate transportation

1963   March on Washington for Jobs and Freedom

1965   Selma to Montgomery (Alabama) march for voting rights for Black citizens

1965   March on Washington to End the Vietnam War

1965   Gay and lesbian rights march at the White House

1966   March of Mexican American farmworkers from Sacramento to Delano (California)

1968   Poor People's Campaign in Washington, DC

1970   First gay pride parade in New York City

1970   First Earth Day celebration

1971   May Day protests against the Vietnam War

1972   National Aborigines Day protests in Australia

1977   Sit-ins at government buildings by the American Coalition of Citizens with Disabilities

1978   The "Longest Walk" from San Francisco to Washington, DC, by Native Americans demanding treaty rights

1978   March for the Equal Rights Amendment in Washington, DC

1979   First National March on Washington for Lesbian and Gay Rights

1981   Solidarity Day March for labor unions in Washington, DC

1982   March and rally for nuclear disarmament in New York City

1984   Sit-ins in Washington, DC, protesting apartheid in South Africa

1987   Start of protests by the AIDS Coalition to Unleash Power (ACT UP)

1988   "Survival Day" march by Aboriginal and Torres Strait islander people seeking rights in Australia

1989   Mass protests against the wall dividing East Berlin from West Berlin

1990 "Capitol Crawl" protest in Washington, DC, demanding passage of the Americans with Disabilities Act

1990 Nationwide rallies against the Gulf War

1992 March for Women's Lives in Washington, DC

2002 Nationwide protests against the War on Terror

2003 Freedom Rides for immigrant workers

2006 Founding of the Me Too movement for survivors of sexual abuse, especially girls and women of color

2010 First Arab Spring demonstrations against oppressive governments across the Arab world

2013 Founding of Black Lives Matter, a movement seeking social justice for Black people

2016 Standing Rock reservation encampment against the construction of the Dakota Access Pipeline

2017 Women's March in Washington, DC, and in more than eight hundred locations worldwide

2018 March for Our Lives, in DC and across the nation, protesting gun violence in schools

2019 School Strike 4 Climate, a worldwide demonstration led by Greta Thunberg and others

2019 Nationwide rallies for immigrants and Dreamers, undocumented people brought to the United States as children

2020 Nationwide protests for racial justice, sparked by the murders of George Floyd, Breonna Taylor, and others

2021 Nationwide protests against the discrimination faced by Asian Americans

Text © 2021 Michael G. Long
Illustrations © 2021 Carlos Vélez

First edition
Published by Flyaway Books
Louisville, Kentucky

21 22 23 24 25 26 27 28 29 30–10 9 8 7 6 5 4 3 2 1

Book design by Allison Taylor

PRINTED IN CHINA

Most Flyaway Books are available at special quantity discounts when purchased in bulk by corporations, organizations, and special-interest groups. For more information, please e-mail SpecialSales@flyawaybooks.com.

Library of Congress Cataloging-in-Publication Data
Names: Long, Michael G., author. | Vélez, Carlos, 1980- illustrator.
Title: Three lines in a circle : the exciting life of the peace symbol / written by Michael G. Long ; illustrated by Carlos Vélez.
Description: First edition. | Louisville, Kentucky : Flyaway Books, [2021] | Audience: Ages 3-7. | Audience: Grades K-1. | Summary: Relates the story of the peace symbol--designed in 1958 by Gerry Holtom, a London activist protesting nuclear weapons--and how it inspires people all over the world, from peace marches and liberation movements to the end of apartheid and the fall of the Berlin Wall. Includes a short history of the peace symbol and a partial timeline of peaceful protests since 1958.

Identifiers: LCCN 2021009020 (print) | LCCN 2021009021 (ebook) | ISBN 9781947888326 (hardback) | ISBN 9781646981960 (ebook)
Subjects: CYAC: Peace symbol--Fiction. | Holtom, Gerald--Fiction.
Classification: LCC PZ7.1.L6654 Th 2021 (print) | LCC PZ7.1.L6654 (ebook) | DDC [E]--dc23
LC record available at https://lccn.loc.gov/2021009020
LC ebook record available at https://lccn.loc.gov/2021009021